Let's Go!

Michael Emberley

I Like to Read® COMICS

HOLIDAY HOUSE • NEW YORK

Got it!

What is it?
It's a party!
Can we go?
YES!
Come to a PARTY!
When: Today
Time: Soon!

LET'S GO!

Too slow!
Now what do we do?
I know!

Help me.

Help me.

Ready?

LET'S GO!

Uh-oh!
Snow!
Now what do we do?

I KNOW!
Ready?

Here we go!
Away we go!

Down we go!
Let's go!
Go!

Uh-oh!
Whoa!
No more snow.

Oh...
no...
here...
we go...
again.
Now what do we do?

I KNOW!
?
?
Now watch this.

Keep going.

Everybody ready?

Let's go!

5

Oh no!

Oh no!

In we go!

Now what do we do?
I know!

Look.

Help me.
It works!

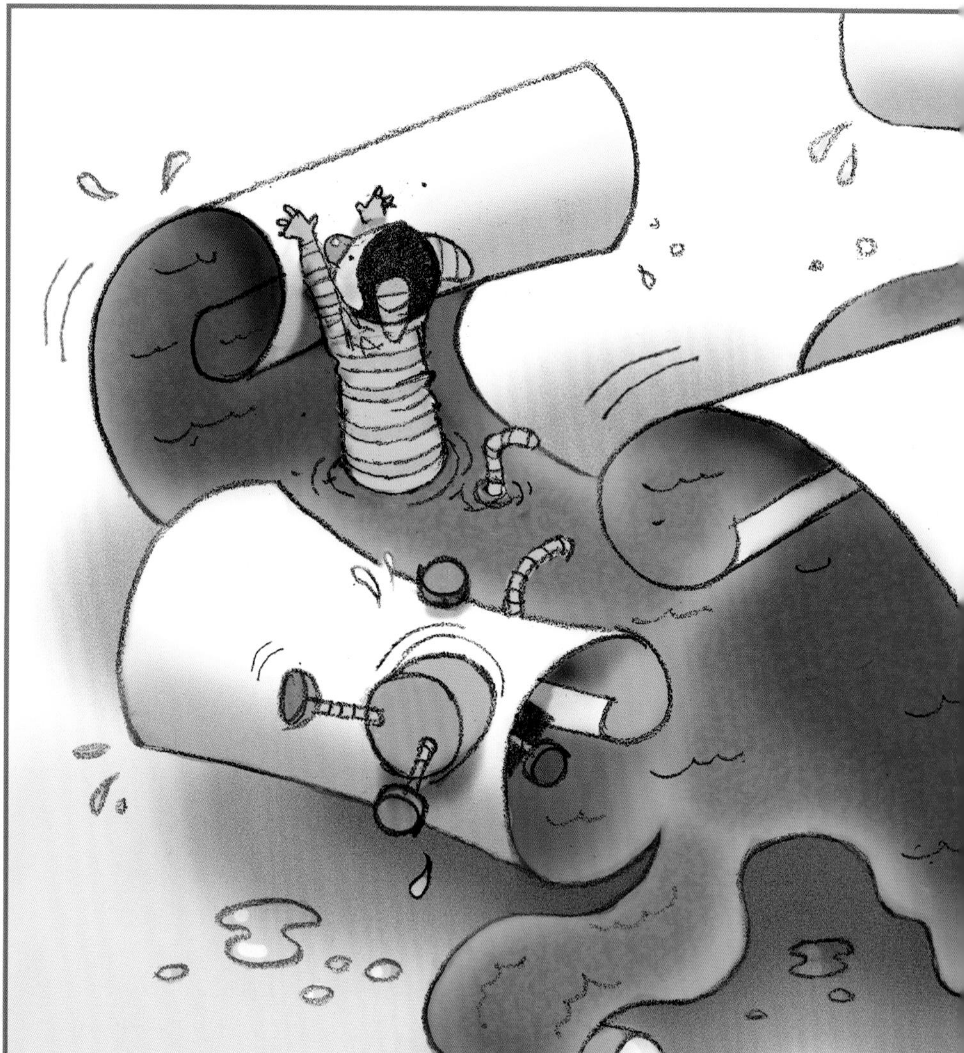

Now what?
I know!

Knock-
knock!
Hey!
Hello?
You’re here!

Come in!

LET'S PARTY!

Cool hat!
Thanks.
Let's make hats!
What a great PARTY!
Are you going?
It's late.
I know.

LET'S STAY!